WORLD WILDLIFE FUND

Look Who's

Published in 1998 by Cedco Publishing Company,
100 Pelican Way, San Rafael, CA 94901.
Produced by Jennifer Barry Design, Sausalito, CA.

For a free catalog of our entire line of books, write us at the address above,
visit our website: www.cedco.com or e-mail us at: sales@cedco.com

Photography Credits
front cover: ©Van Nostrand, Photo Researchers
title page: ©Richard Day, Daybreak Imagery
page 6,7: ©Wolfgang Kaehler
page 8,9: ©Van Nostrand, Photo Researchers
page 11: ©Dwight Kuhn
page 12-15: ©Fred Bavendam
page 17, cover flap: ©Gerry Ellis, ENP Images; under flap: ©Kevin Schafer
page 18,19: ©Michael & Patricia Fogden
page 20,21: ©Steve Gettle, ENP Images
page 23: ©Brian Kenney
page 24,25: ©Leonard Rue III, Photo Researchers
page 26,27: ©Art Wolfe
page 29: ©Richard Day, Daybreak Imagery

Some photographs have been digitally-manipulated to produce this book.

Hatching!

My nest's on the rocks

and I live where it's cold.

Look who's hatching!

Penguin Chick

My nest's inside
a rotting log,
and I slither through
the forest.
Look who's hatching!

My nest's an **anemone** and

I grow up in a coral reef.

Look who's hatching!

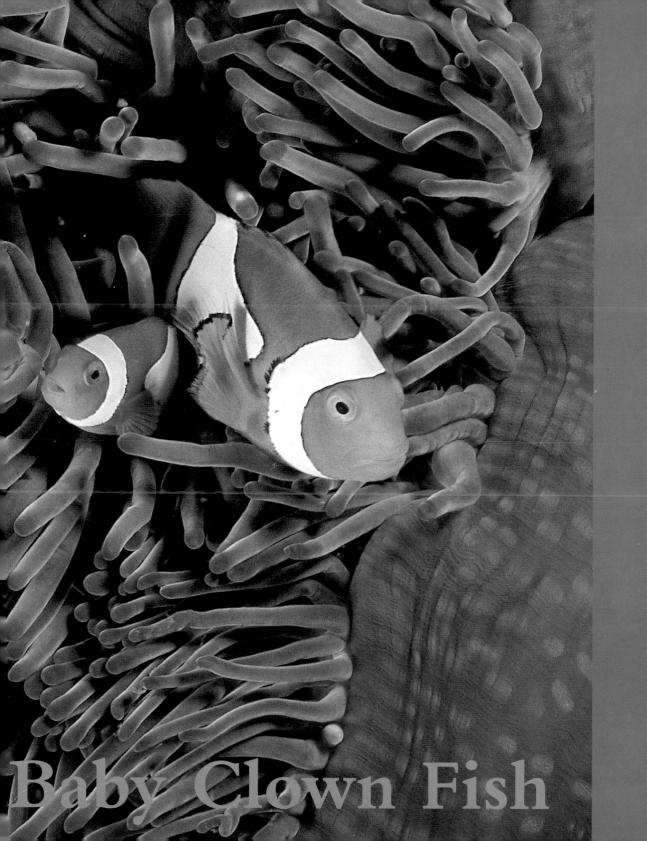

Baby Clown Fish

My nest's in a sandy hole, and I swim in the sea. Look who's hatching!

My nest's on a leaf and

I can cling to the trees.

Look who's hatching!

Baby Tree Frog

My nest's on the riverbank, and I live on both the water and land. Look who's hatching!

My nest's in the grass and

I'm a **bird** that can't fly.

Look who's hatching!

My nest's in
the trees,
and my eggs are
pale blue.

Look who's hatching!